THE ALIEN'S SURPRISE

GRACE KENSINGTON

1

____

"I think that's going to be enough, Babe," Ty said, taking another loaf of bread from Samira's hand and shoving it down into the bag sitting on the counter, "There's going to be food on the trail."

"Can you be absolutely sure of that?" Samira asked, her eyes sparkling with the tears that she was fighting to hold back, "You have no idea what's out there. Can you be absolutely positive that when you walk out of this compound that you are actually going to be able to find enough food to keep you going while you are away?"

Ty looked at his mate rushing around his bakery, gathering the loaves of bread she had baked for him, and felt his heart constrict. The truth was that he really didn't have any idea what it was going to be like when he and the Denynso warriors left the compound to go explore Uoria and find out what types of species, plants, and land existed outside of the small area of land that they had always occupied. Their kind had never left the compound and had existed completely within their small area of the planet without really considering what might be going on outside their boundaries.

When they fought the wars that made them famous around the galaxy as the most fearsome and aggressive warriors in existence, it was against species that came to their planet and infiltrated their space.

It was one of these battles that had made them realize the desperate need to get outside of their compound and explore. In that battle, the final and brutal clash with their long-time enemies the KIimnu, they discovered that there was an entire realm right beneath their feet, a mirror of the land that existed above it, that had been home to a species that they had never even known was there. The idea that a species of creatures had lived right under their compound as long as they had been there without any of the Denynso, not even the king, even knowing that they were there was terrifying, and they realized that they would never be able to protect themselves or their families properly if they didn't know what was going on on the rest of the planet.

Now the warriors along with Ty, the nurturer and baker of the tribe, and Ciyrs, the healer, would be leaving the next morning on a quest that would take them into the furthest unknown regions of the planet so that they may make contact with other creatures and find out what else grew and existed on their planet. It was a frightening prospect, one that could be extremely beneficial to the Denynso and the humans that had come to live with them, or one that could put their entire clan, compound, and existence in danger.

Ty watched Samira draw a small paper-wrapped package out from under the counter and place it in front of her. His heart squeezed even harder as he looked at her, her shoulders trembling as she couldn't hold back the tears any longer. He knew that his mate, this beautiful human woman that had been the biggest surprise in his life and the greatest thing that ever happened to him when she appeared just weeks before, was worried about him and his safety as he embarked on this journey. If he gave himself the time to really think about it, he would probably be worried about it, too.

He needed to do this, though. It was only recently, and through the support and love that Samira poured out to him from the moment that she met him was the reason he had been able to fully embrace who he was and the power that he had within him. His entire life the large, imposing Denynso man had focused entirely on taking care of the clan. He was the one who made sure that they had the food that they needed and that they recovered after battles. He was not a warrior. He had not been born to be one. A treasured, unique power he had inherited from his father and that he had hidden deep within him from the time he was a child, had proven that he was more than just a nurturer. Through uncovering and embracing that power he was able to step into the role of a warrior and join the ranks of the others as they marched into the final showdown with the Klimnu. It was his ability to move and control objects with his thoughts that had enabled him to be a powerful and unexpected force against the slimy, disgusting creatures that had been the bane of the existence of his kind for generations.

Now he needed to offer that same support and help to the warriors as they went out into the world to try to understand it better, and find more ways that they could not only improve the life they had, but to also protect themselves into the future. Samira had completely changed everything for him, and he was unwilling to let her be in danger if there was anything he could do to change it. They already planned on going back to Earth after the quest to marry the way that humans did, further solidifying the bond that had connected them as lifelong mates within the Denynso tribe. He couldn't in good conscious let himself do that if he didn't know that he could bring his wife and the potential future mother of his children back to a place that was safe.

"What's that?" he asked softly, trying to calm her with his voice.

"I made it for you," she said, sliding the package closer to him, "I've been working on it since right after we bonded. I just finished it last night."

Ty released the twine she had tied into a bow on the top of the package and unwrapped the thick brown paper. Inside was a complex-looking box comprised of gears and metal components. A small dip in the top caught his attention. He ran his finger across it and looked up at Samira.

"What is it?" he asked.

Samira smiled now, the expression a welcome break from the tears that streamed down her face and made her large eyes look deep and sad. She reached into her pocket and withdrew something, clutching it tightly in her hand. Taking a deep breath, she turned her hand over and opened her palm, holding it out toward him. Nestled in the middle of her palm was a gold ring, the metal antiqued and the design complex and beautiful. A series of prongs in the center held a dark red gem.

"I know that you probably don't know this because there's no reason that you should, but on Earth when people get engaged the girl usually wears a ring. It is just part of the whole ritual. Then both of them wear bands when they actually get married. Well, this was my great-grandmother's engagement ring and it was passed down through the family to me. I thought that since we are doing things a little differently than other human women are, that maybe I could give you an engagement ring instead."

Feeling tears starting to prick painfully in his own eyes, Ty took the ring from her palm and looked at it closely. Even though Samira was taller and larger than all of the other human women except for Zuri, the ring was still too small even to fit on Ty's pinky. She giggled when he tried to push it down toward the first knuckle of his pinky.

"No. It's not for you to wear," she said, "Let me show you."

She took the ring from him and nestled it down into the dip on the top of the metal box she had given him. As soon as it settled into place, the gears started to turn and Ty heard her voice coming through to him, telling him that she loved him and missed him and couldn't wait to have him home.

"This is incredible," he said when her voice stopped.

He was in such awe of her. He knew that Samira was incredibly brilliant and that it was the reason she had come to Uoria in the first place, as a way to expand her knowledge and to help the Denynso healer Ciyrs create healing oint-ments for the warriors, but it still stunned him. She was so young, and yet her beautiful, graceful hands were able to create something like this.

"If you push the button on the bottom, there are a few more of the voice discs that you can play. Just take out the ring, twist this top panel counter clockwise until it releases, lift it up, remove the disc that is in there, put in a different one, twist the panel back into place, and then put the ring back in and it will play just like that."

"Oh, just like that, huh?" Ty asked.

Samira laughed and looked down shyly. She often forgot how smart she was and that other people weren't able to understand the things that she did with almost no effort.

"If I were you, I'd listen to those discs by yourself the first time. There are a couple of them that may not be... appropriate for the other warriors to hear."

"Oh, really?" Ty said, lowering the box back onto the surface of the counter and walking around to Samira.

He slipped his arms around her waist and started guiding her backwards toward the door to their house, taking off his bag and putting it on the counter as they went.

2
___

"The way I see it, this trip can't be any more difficult than going all the way to Earth to find you and getting into it with Samira's stepfather," Ero said, cuddling closer to Zuri.

"At least when you went to Earth, you knew what you were getting yourself into," she said, wrapping an arm around his waist and tugging him closer.

"No, I didn't," Ero protested, "I didn't know anything about Earth other than that you were there. None of us had ever been there. In fact, none of us had ever been in a spaceship. I was so worried about not ever seeing you again that it didn't really matter to me that I was going to a completely different planet that I didn't know what it looked like or how I would make my way around. I hadn't met too many humans in my life, and most of the ones that I had were not exactly pleasant."

"Were you scared?"

Ero thought about the question carefully. He didn't really know how to answer. He was being totally honest when he said that it didn't matter to him when he climbed on that ship that he was going all the way to Earth to find her, but when he thought back on it he knew that it wasn't so much that it didn't frighten him, but that it didn't matter to him that he was frightened. It had been his fault that Zuri had left Uoria only twenty-four hours after she had arrived with the intention of being the first professor to come to the planet to be a part of the exchange program the king, Creia, had planned with the university on Earth. He had hurt her so badly with a comment that he made about her to the other warriors that she had left, even after they had bonded for the first time. It was his responsibility to go after her and convince her that he loved her and needed her to come back to Uoria with him to be his mate. It still seemed like an unimaginable gift that she actually had.

"I know that you don't want me to go, but isn't this exactly what you wanted to do when you came here?" he asked.

Zuri gave a huff as if he had put voice to something that she had been trying to avoid.

"I don't think that's really applicable."

Ero laughed.

"Really?" he said, tickling her playfully, "You don't think it's the same thing that you wanted to know everything you could about the Denynso and to teach us about humans so you came to be a part of the exchange program? Actually, you know what? You're right. It's not the same. You came all the way from another planet to find out more about Uoria and the Denynso. I'm just leaving the compound."

"It's not the same thing. There have been scientists coming to Uoria to study for years. I at least had some kind of idea of what I was getting myself into when I came here. I knew I was coming to a specific compound to interact with a certain species. I definitely didn't have all of the information or know exactly what the Denynso were like, but at least I had a few reference points. You have absolutely no clue what you are walking into. You are literally just going out and wandering around on a planet that not a single member of your kind has ever walked around on, essentially just hoping that whatever you find is not going to kill you. I'm sorry if I don't find that terribly comforting."

Ero lifted up on his elbow and gazed down into Zuri's face. Her thick blond hair rippled around her lovely, round face, still flushed, and her bare shoulders. Large blue eyes gazed up at him and he had to take a moment just to look at her. His mate was truly the most beautiful woman he had ever seen and part of him still couldn't believe that she was really his.

"This is something that I have to do, my love."

"But why?"

"Well, not only is it my responsibility and my duty as a warrior of the Denynso, but I have been thinking a lot about the future and what it might hold for us. I don't want to get to that point knowing that I didn't do absolutely everything that I could to make sure that our future is safe and happy as possible."

"What point?" Zuri asked.

Her voice had become soft and when he looked into her eyes he knew that she knew what he was thinking about, but needed to hear him say it. Ero rested his hand on Zuri's stomach and rubbed it gently, looking down to watch his palm follow the curves of her belly and the swell of her hipbones.

"When we will have a little one of our own. Seeing Pyra and Eden get ready for their baby has made me think about how wonderful it would be to see you carrying our child, and to get to be a father. I didn't have a chance to have a good relationship with my father growing up to really make any memories with him, and I know that I want to be able to do that for someone."

Even though his parents had died when Ero was very young, talking about them and the relationship with them that he had missed out on throughout his life brought the same deep sadness that it always had. He had always been the orphan of the Denynso, but also the smallest among the warriors. These factors had combined to give him a bitter, angry attitude and a propensity for distrust and violence as he got older. The other warriors had never missed the opportunity to tease and bully him about his size, and it was this bullying that had pushed him to the cruel comments he had made about Zuri. It had been the horrible moment when he realized what he did to her that it finally occurred to him truly how deeply the teasing had impacted him. When he saw the painful look in her eyes he saw all of the hurt that he had experienced and knew that he had just done the exact same thing to her that the warriors had done to him all those years.

Zuri let out a long breath and rested her hand over Ero's on her stomach.

"I've been thinking about that, too," she admitted.

Ero grinned and rolled over onto her, capturing her mouth with his and exploring her with his tongue. He pressed into her, hoping that he would be able to memorize the feeling of every inch of her body beneath him when he was away and lonely for her.

"Let's get started now," he growled into her ear and Zuri laughed.

Ero felt her hands pushing on his shoulders and he complied with the pressure, letting her ease her back onto his side on the bed.

"Hold on there," she said, rolling out from under the blankets, "Let me give you this first."

Ero groaned in protest as she got out of bed, but let himself enjoy watching her naked form wiggling its way across the room to the desk against the wall. He let out a grunt of appreciation when she bent over to look in the drawer and Zuri glanced over her shoulder at him. She smiled before straightening and making her way back over to the bed so that she could hand him what looked like a large book.

"What's this?"

"It's a field journal. I brought it with me from the university and I want you to bring it with you on your trip. I planned on recording all of my observations about the Denynso in it so that I could present them to the university board when I went back. "

"We're just like big giant specimens to you, aren't we?" Ero teased.

"Yes. You're my favorite, though."

Zuri leaned over and kissed him. Ero tossed the journal over to the bedside table. He was happy that he would have it with him when he left the compound and needed to feel her with him, but in that moment she was there, close enough for him to touch and kiss, and he was going to take absolute advantage of it.

3

———

Eden ran her hand down the back of Pyra's head, stroking the long white hair that he usually wore in the customary Mohawk of the Denynso men but was now laying soft. His breath tickled on her bare skin as he whispered to her belly, but it was so sweet that she didn't want to giggle and stop him before he was finished. He was explaining to their baby why he had to leave and that he was going to get back as soon as he could.

"I just want you to be safe," he whispered, running his hand along the side of her belly as he spoke, "and that means I have to go out there and find out if there are any scary things that I will have to fight off for you. I don't want you to worry about me. You just stay in there and concentrate on getting all big and strong. I'll be just fine and when you're ready, you'll come out and we'll run and play and I'll teach you how to climb a tree."

Eden laughed then and her enormous mate looked up at her.

"What?"

"I don't think that climbing a tree is something that will

happen directly after birth." She stopped, realizing that there were still many things that no one knew about her pregnancy or the baby that she was carrying, "Right? I mean, this will be a baby, right? Like a small baby. Not a toddler that will be able to get up and walk around right after birth?"

Pyra returned her laugh and stroked her belly again.

"I don't think so, Babe. I, for one, have never actually seen one, but I'm fairly certain that Denynso babies are small and baby-like. I don't think walking around is a thing for a couple of years, but that doesn't mean that I can't start planning now."

He leaned down and kissed the swell of her belly, closing his eyes briefly. Eden could feel his hand pressing more firmly into her skin as if he were trying to get close enough to the baby to touch it even through her body.

"You can plan anything you want. He's going to be yours."

Pyra sat up sharply and looked directly into her face.

"He?" he asked.

Eden immediately regretted what she had said. She had been so careful not to say that, but now there was no way that she could just scoop the words out of the air and put them back into her mouth. He had already heard them.

"I don't know for sure," Eden said cautiously, drawing out each of her words as carefully as she could to make sure that Pyra heard her and understood what she was saying. She didn't want him to get his hopes up when she wasn't entirely sure that she believed it herself, "The midwives don't have any way of knowing what the baby is."

"Then why did you say 'he'?"

Eden sighed. She wasn't sure how her mate was going to respond to her little experiment with Loralia a few days before. It wasn't the custom of the Denynso to try to find out what a baby was before it was born, but when the strange and mysterious creature who had come from the mirrored realm beneath the compound told her that she could tell her what her baby was going to be, Eden's curiosity had simply been too much for her and she couldn't say no.

"When the girls and I went over to Bannack's house the other night to meet with Loralia, she was telling us about her kind. She was fascinated by my belly and she asked if I knew if the baby was a boy or a girl. I told her that the midwives didn't have any way of finding that out, but I mentioned that if I was going through my pregnancy on Earth, my doctors would be able to tell me what it was."

"They could?" he asked, seeming both fascinated and a bit upset that this was not something that was available on his planet.

"Yes. So she told me that she would be able to tell me."

Eden thought about the gorgeous and completely unexpected woman that was Loralia. The very last of her kind, she had been living in the hidden realm under the compound her entire life, but had been alone for many years. When the young, impulsive warrior Bannack brought her up into the compound it had been the first time that she had ever been above the surface of the ground. Though she hadn't had the opportunity to spend much time with her, Eden had felt a connection with this misunderstood creature, and was thrilled that she and Bannack were now mated.

Pyra had been staring at her expectantly, but Eden was still unsure whether she wanted to tell him what Loralia had said.

"And?" Pyra said, widening his eyes like he was trying to encourage her forward, "What exactly did she say?"

He looked so excited that Eden couldn't help but smile.

"She put her mirror against my belly and told me that the baby is a boy."

Pyra looked delighted and he bounded to the head of the bed to gather Eden in a tight hug.

"A boy? Really?"

"Yes. She said he will be a strong warrior just like you."

"I'm so excited," he said, rubbing her belly again, "I mean, I would have loved a daughter, too, but having a son..."

His voice trailed off as if the emotion he was feeling was just too much to try to condense into words. Eden felt a surge of pride at that moment that was difficult to explain. She loved that she was carrying her mate's baby, and that she had the privilege of being the mother to the first of the new generation of Denynso, but watching Pyra at that moment as he slithered back down the bed and rested his mouth to her belly again, it all felt even more meaningful. Giving Pyra a son felt like the most important, precious, and valuable thing that she had ever done, and she felt so blessed to be able to do it, even if she was still somewhat fearful of the unknown about her pregnancy.

"My son," Pyra whispered against her skin, "My boy. Your Papa loves you, little one."

Eden reached carefully under her pillow, trying not to disturb Pyra as he continued to whisper to the baby, and took out the braided ribbon chain she had been keeping there. On it was a pendant cast from iron that looked like a hand cradling a heart in its palm. A smaller heart in the center of the larger heart featured an inlay of copper so that it stood out against the other pieces.

"I want you to bring this with you," she said to Pyra and he sat up, looking from her face to the pendant in her hand,

"I designed it a couple of weeks after I found out I was pregnant. Jem," she paused and choked back the painful emotion that suddenly tightened in her throat at the mention of the warrior who had died in the recent battle with the Klimnu, "crafted it for me."

A brilliant blacksmith, Jem had taken her vision for the pendant that would represent Pyra holding her and their baby and crafted it into something so beautiful it had taken her breath away when she saw it. She had intended to give it to Pyra when the baby was born, but now that he was leaving with the other warriors, she wanted him to take it with him so that he could have them close to him even while he was far away.

Pyra took the pendant from her hand and ran his massive fingers along the design.

"Thank you," he said softly, "I can't tell you how much I am going to miss you. I feel like I'm not going to be able to breathe without you."

"I'm going to miss you, too," Eden said, "I can't bear the thought of sleeping in this big bed without you. I'm going to be alone more nights with you gone on this journey than I was when I first got here before we bonded."

The mention of their first bonding brought a flash of heat to her cheeks. That had been such a tumultuous, emotional time, but as Pyra lifted up to lie down beside her and pull Eden in against her so that he could cradle her in his arms, she knew that she would never trade a single second of it.

4

____

Leia's hand clutched at the sheets beside her, her knuckles clenching so hard into the fabric that they whitened as she pulled it away from the mattress. Her eyes closed as her head dropped back against the pillow and her back arched up off of the bed. Gyyx flattened one massive hand into the middle of her chest and pressed her back down, holding her against the mattress with just enough pressure that she could feel his dominance. This sent even more of a shiver of excitement and arousal through her and she couldn't hold back the cry of pleasure as her mate flicked his tongue through her hot, wet folds again.

Gyyx had spread her thighs against the bed and pushed them up so that she was fully open to him, making her totally vulnerable to his touch. He pushed them up a little higher now, using the very tip of his tongue to concentrate fast, intense strokes directly on the pearl of hypersensitive flesh just at her peak. The sensation rolled through her like thunder, sending nearly overwhelming ripples of pleasure all the way along her body. Leia writhed against the bed, but

Gyyx was far larger and far stronger than she was, and the pressure of his hands ensured that she would stay exactly where he wanted her for as long as he wanted her to stay there.

Of course, there was nowhere else that she would want to be in that moment. She reveled in being at her mate's mercy and in the way that he could so masterfully manipulate her body to create feelings within her that she had never experienced before.

Just as Leia felt like she was going to lose all control, Gyyx pulled his tongue away from her body and pressed a series of soft kisses along the inside of her thigh. He was allowing her to cool, to come down from the spiraling heights of pleasure he was sending her into so that he could just bring her right back there again. It was delicious, delirious torture.

She felt him guide her legs down and his hand slide from her chest down to one of her hands so that he could ease her up to a sitting position. As he did this, Gyyx came around to her side, changing positions with her so that he lay with his head on the pillow and guided her to kneel in between his slightly spread legs. Leia bit down on her bottom lip as the position brought her right into view of his powerful erection. Her mouth watered as she looked at it and she couldn't resist running her tongue from its base to the tip. There was already a crystalline drop of fluid collected there and she licked it up, allowing the tip of her tongue to dip inside just briefly.

Gripping the base of his cock in one hand, Leia traced the edge of the crown with her tongue, pausing for a moment to concentrate her licks on the bundle of nerves on the underside of the head just as he had concentrated on her. As Gyyx began to groan beneath her, Leia started to stroke with the hand that was holding him, gliding her palm and fingers along his hard, thick length as she continued to memorize his ridges and veins with the tip of her tongue. The taste of his body made her shiver, making her want him even more.

Suddenly Gyyx sat up and grabbed Leia by her upper arms, turning her and laying her down on her stomach so that she faced the foot of the bed. He climbed over her, balancing on his hands and the balls of his feet so that he didn't press too much of his tremendous body down on her tiny frame, and she felt his erection gliding along her thighs as he rolled his hips to stroke against her without entering her. Leia whimpered and lifted her hips, displaying herself to encourage him to fulfill the ache within her that he had created with the skilled ministrations of his tongue.

Gyyx complied suddenly, pushing deeply inside her in one hard thrust that elicited a scream of pleasure from deep in Leia's chest. The warrior growled and lay forward so that Leia could feel his body full enveloping hers. It was a primal, comforting feeling that encouraged her to lift her hips and grind them into him. His hands came up under her, cupping at the front of her throat in another show of dominance that made Leia feel so close to the edge that two more hard thrusts sent her body shuddering through an intense orgasm that left her gasping for breath.

Her climax did nothing to slow Gyyx. Instead, he tightened his grip around her throat so that her back arched slightly and pulled up onto his knees for better leverage so that he could slam in her with such speed and depth that each stroke was almost painful. That fine line between pain and pleasure, however, is what drove Leia crazy and she let the sounds pour out of her, panting, gasping, and crying out as she gave her body over to Gyyx in the hopes that he would still be able to feel her when he was gone.

Suddenly she felt his entire body tense and heard him let out a strangled moan as his cock pulsed wildly within her. He stayed buried deeply inside her as the tremors continued to flow through him, spilling hot streams that she could feel filling her. Finally he lowered his hands from her throat to her chest and carefully rolled them over to their sides, remaining inside her as he curled around her.

Even though she would have liked him to, Gyyx never let himself collapse down on top of Leia. She was so small and delicate-looking, particularly compared to him, that he was always convinced he would crush her if he let himself rest on top of her completely. Instead, he curved around her, cradling her body close to his so that she was surrounded by his warmth and the intoxicating smell of his skin.

His lips touched her neck and traveled up, following the curve of her jaw until he reached her ear.

"I love you," he breathed, pulling her a little closer to his chest and stomach.

"I love you, too," she said back, kissing the arm that was draped tightly around her.

Leia couldn't help but smile as she allowed herself to drift away on the waves of pleasure still rolling through her. It had taken so much to convince Gyyx that he was not going to break her if he made love to her the way that she wanted him to, but now that they had bonded, he had stepped into the dominant, aggressive role that drove her wild and brought out every primal instinct within her. She loved his strength and his power, and the way he knew how to use them to give her such incredible pleasure. She felt fully and completely safe with him, which made it even better when he exerted himself so strongly.

When their bodies had relaxed and cooled, she carefully extracted herself from his arms and walked over to the large black artist's bag she had propped against the wall. Reaching inside the main pocket, she withdrew what looked like a small scroll. She brought it over to the bed and climbed under the covers to meet his body where he had also cuddled down into the bed.

"This is for you to bring with you so that you can look at it and think of me whenever you're lonely."

Gyyx took the scroll from her and unrolled it carefully. She heard him let out a sigh as he saw the picture.

"This is beautiful, Leia," he said, turning to kiss her tenderly, "Thank you."

"I wanted to frame it for you, but then I figured that you probably weren't going to have the space in your bag to bring along a framed picture, and even if you did, you weren't really going to be able to find a place to hang it while you were traveling around." She looked down at the picture and reached over to run her fingers along the pencil and acrylic sketch. "This is the sunrise that I saw the first morning that I knew you. I remember it being the most beautiful sunrise I had ever seen, and I know that that's because it was the first one I had ever seen now that I knew you existed in the world."

Gyyx tucked his hand around her face and stared into her eyes. She saw intense emotion there, and she knew that he was worried about her. Them coming together was a difficult and nearly tragic experience that neither of them liked to talk about very much, but both knew was something that was lingering right around them. They had found each other only because the Klimnu had high-jacked the university shuttle she had ridden from Earth, kidnapped her, and help her captive, torturing and tormenting her, for 57 days in a dark, dank prison on the other side of the compound, in one of the areas so close to the edge of their territory that many barely considered it the compound and others would never even venture. This is what compelled him more than anything to join up with the other warriors in order to go out onto the planet and find out what other creatures Uoria might harbor.

"I will think about you every single minute while I'm gone," he said.

"No, you won't," Leia said, kissing the tip of his nose, "'and that's perfectly fine. There are a lot of other things that you will need to focus your attention on. What matters is that you know I'm thinking about you, too, and when you look at the drawing I want you to know that I love you and can't wait to have you home."

5

Elianna buried her head against Ciyrs's shoulder and held him tightly around his neck as he continued to rock her hips against his. She cradled him inside her body, enveloping him as though protecting him in the most powerful way she knew how. His skin was slick and warm with sweat and she felt it mix with her own as they both came down from their climaxes, maintaining the link between their bodies and allowing their breath to stream and blend between them as they preserved these last precious moments in each other's arms.

She kissed the side of his neck and let out a long sigh that seemed to pull with it all of the emotion that she had experienced since coming to Uoria. It had been like nothing she had imagined. When she left Earth to come to this strange and barely-known planet it was with the intention of helping humans learn more about Uoria and the Denynso. As a journalist she planned on writing a series of reports that would help to illuminate this species as the people of Earth got accustomed to the idea that the government and the academic sector were planning on not only making direct contact with the species, but cooperating with them. Knowing the reputation of the Denynso as the most powerful and skilled warriors in the galaxy, the goal was to bring some of them to Earth to fight and to train armies, while also allowing humans to go to Uoria to share parts of the Earth culture and visit the planet as tourists.

Elianna had had her own thoughts about these plans, but she had primarily kept them to herself. She wanted to remain as objective as possible, just as her career demanded, and that meant not contemplating a future in which the inhabitants of this far-away planet showed up on Earth and roamed freely, teaching humans to be even more violent and aggressive than they already were, and in which humans flew off to Uoria on cute little family vacations thinking that they would relax and make some fun memories, when they really had no idea what was awaiting them.

When she arrived, however, Elianna's resistance to other people and pain from abandonment in her past had nearly kept her from accepting Ciyrs as her mate. He had been patient with her, though, guiding her through the difficult and confusing first moments of their connection that would eventually seal them together. Before they could fully mate, however, a member of the Klimnu had masqueraded as Pyra and stolen her, bringing her to a dark, disgusting prison just on the edge of the compound, a place where she would learn that the Denynso never went. There she was tormented and tortured, the only comfort she got came in thinking about Ciyrs and reaching out to him through her mind.

It wasn't until the Denynso came for her that she discovered he had transferred some of his incredible healing power to her, but with the ability to heal came the ability to destroy. As much as she wouldn't want to admit it, she had delighted in the ability to wrap her hand around the bony, slimy neck of the vicious creatures who had made her life a living hell for the entire time that she had been there, and had nearly killed the frail, tiny woman that she had found battered and bloody, crawling through the halls of the prison, and watch them burn.

This had changed her forever. Suddenly life was not about writing articles and bringing back information to the people of Earth so that they could learn more about a planet that would remain a novelty. It became learning about the people that were now her family, giving herself over completely to the man that she loved and who she knew was her lifelong mate, and offering the gifts that she had just discovered to helping heal and protect the Denynso.

Now as she wrapped herself around Ciyrs, reveling in the feeling of the only man who had ever been inside her, she couldn't imagine a single moment of her life without him or without Uoria. She felt more at home and at peace here than she ever had on Earth, and it was as if his presence and the abundant, never-ending love that he gave to her had soothed all of the pain and emptiness she had suffered throughout her life. The thought that he was leaving with the warriors to explore the planet was gut-wrenching and she didn't want to think about it. She wanted to continue to hold him and let him protect her in his massive arms, ignoring the eventuality, and pushing back that moment when he would have to say goodbye.

Suddenly the first rays of sunlight started trickling through the slight gap between the curtains over their bedroom window and she knew that she couldn't put it off any longer. Her mate, the healer of the clan, was a vital component of this mission and he would still need to gather all of his supplies so that he could meet with the warriors at the main hall to be ready to leave after breakfast.

She climbed off of him slowly, savoring the feeling of his body stroking against hers as it left her, and crossed to the bureau on the far wall to pull out a dress that she dropped over her head. Out of a small drawer in the bottom of the piece of furniture she pulled a book tied with a green ribbon. When she turned back around Ciyrs was tying the strings at the front of his pants. She waited while he put on the rest of his clothing, and then stepped forward to hand the book to him.

"I brought this notebook with me from Earth. It was supposed to be where I was going to make my notes for my articles, but after I met you, I realized that I was never going to go back there so I didn't need to write them. Instead, you gave me the confidence to do something that I had never told anyone that I wanted to do, but that I had been dreaming of for my entire life."

Cirys untied the ribbon and lifted the hard front cover of the notebook. She watched him read the first few lines of her neat, precise handwriting and then look up at her.

"What is this?"

"I wrote a book. It's not quite finished yet, but I want you to bring it with you and read it. You'll be the very first person to read anything that I've written other than articles, and you can help me decide how to end it."

Ciyrs gathered Elianna into his arms and hugged her close to him. She breathed in the smell of his body and listened to the rhythm of his heart, wanting to internalize that sound so that she could replay it in her mind whenever she thought of him while he was gone.

"I will be thinking about you every day. I'll get home as soon as I can."

"I know you will."

As Ciyrs released her, she glanced down at the bed. It was going to be next to impossible to sleep without him beside her. The bed looked so big, empty, and cold already and she dreaded nightfall when she would have to climb in and try to will herself to sleep alone.

"Come to the shop and help me pack up the healing ointments and other supplies?" he asked.

Elianna nodded and let him take her hand, intertwining their fingers as he led her out of their house and through the compound toward the building that held his shop and clinic. This was where they healed the sick and injured, and where they had worked with Ty's brilliant mate Samira to create powerful healing ointments that had gotten them through the last battles with the Klimnu. She knew that the bottles and tubes that he packed in his large bag would be integral to the trip, but she didn't want to think of the suffering that they would end.

As they packed his supplies and checked the list of items that he had made the day before, Elianna could hear the compound outside coming to life as the Denynso started heading for the meeting hall to eat breakfast and say final goodbyes to the men.

6

———

"I can't believe that I just found you, and now I have to leave you."

Bannack tightened his hands around Loralia's and stared into her still-startling lavender eyes. He had spent only three days with her, and one of them had been spent trying to find her so that he could apologize and convince her to come back with him. Now he was going to be walking away from her, leaving her in a strange place that she didn't know so that he could explore the rest of the planet for an indeterminate amount of time. Though it had been his idea in the first place for the warriors to go outside of the compound and explore Uoria to find out what other types of species existed beyond their boundaries, now that he was only minutes away from leaving, it made his stomach feel sick.

"Everything is going to be fine," Loralia soothed him, stroking the tip of his nose with hers, "You are going to go and discover amazing new things, and I will be here getting used to my new home. The women have been very kind to me and I'm sure that they will continue to do everything that they can to make me feel welcome and to help me assimilate to life up here."

His mate was truly incredible and Bannack couldn't help but stare at her in amazement. This creature, the last of her kind, had not only lived completely on her own without any contact from other species for years after her family and friends died from a mysterious plague that had spared only her for reasons that even she didn't understand, but had also left the only home that she had ever known in order to come above ground and be his mate among a strange species and in a world that she had never experienced. He might be a warrior, but Loralia by far had more courage than he ever would.

"I just feel horrible for even suggesting that we go do this so soon after meeting you."

Loralia shook her head.

"This is something that needs to be done. If it wasn't for the bravery and curiosity of the Denynso, the Klimnu never would have been eliminated, and you never would have found me."

"Well," Bannack said, squirming a little against the bench, "technically it wasn't the bravery and curiosity of the Denynso. It was the bravery and curiosity of the human women. They're the ones that went down into the tunnel after we found it, and they're the ones that went back and figured out that the Klimnu were using the mirrored realm to get to us. We just kind of went along with it."

Loralia laughed and Bannack felt his heart soar. He had struggled to think that he was ever going to find a mate, and then when he found her, he had fought even harder against himself, trying to tell himself that he was not the type of person that could mate with a species that was not his own. Of course, that was just his own fear and questions about himself talking and quickly the other warriors and their human mates showed him how wrong he was. He would never be able to thank them enough for pushing him to listen to what was truly in his heart and not what was going through his mind.

"I love you, Bannack," Loralia said, "and when you leave here, you will carry my love with you. But I also want you to bring this."

She reached into the small pouch that she wore on one hip and withdrew what looked like a slightly larger version of the compact that she wore around her neck and that held the mirrors she used to manipulate the space around her. It hung from a chain that looked like it was made of a long braid of her hair. Bannack took the compact into his palm and stared down at it. It didn't shimmer like hers did, but looked heavy and dark like the deeply scrolled metal hadn't been touched in many years.

"This compact," she said, touching it gently with her fingertips, "was my father's. He was an incredible man, and so are you. My hair connects this compact to mine. If you need me, just open the compact and reflect the braid in the top mirror for a few seconds. Mine will let me know that you're calling for me, and when I open my compact I will be able to see anything reflected in yours, and you will be able to see anything reflected in mine."

This was the most amazing gift Bannack could have imagined. He had been struggling knowing that unlike the other warriors and their mates, he was not able to connect with Loralia through her mind and communicate with her through their thoughts. It had made him feel like they weren't as tightly linked as the others, though he knew that he loved her with the same intensity as the other men loved their women. This compact, something that she had treasured for so long, was not just a reminder of her for when they were apart, but also a tangible way for him to connect with her in a manner that was completely unique to them.

"Good morning, everyone."

The deep sound of King Creia's voice brought the attention of everyone in the hall toward the platform where the king and his queen, Theia, stood. They looked out over the clan gathered in the meeting hall with the fondness and pride of parents overlooking their children. Several of the warriors were, in fact, their children, but even those who were not theirs by blood were adored by the kind and caring king and queen.

"This morning is very special for all of us, Creia continued. Today is the first day of a time of discovery that will change the future for every one of us. Through their selflessness, courage, and determination, our warriors and healer will do what no other Denynso has ever been able to do; learn what exists beyond our compound boundaries and what it means for our clan. The journey may be long and difficult, but I have absolute faith and confidence in each one of them that they will be successful and make us all even more proud of them, and of our kind, than we already are. I want each of them to know that our thoughts are with them and that we will all be eagerly awaiting their return. For now, everyone enjoy breakfast and spend some time together. They depart in one hour."

Creia nodded and stepped back, walking down off of the platform with Theia so that they could go to their nearby table and eat. The meeting hall cooks had placed trays overflowing with food into the centers of the long tables and everyone was starting to eat, but Bannack didn't have much of an appetite. He was too busy regretting everything that he had done and said in the first day that he knew Loralia. Though she had forgiven him without question, he felt like he was never going to be able to let go of those lost moments with her.

"Don't hate yourself, Bannack," Loralia said.

Though she couldn't read his thoughts the way that the other mates could read the thoughts of their Denynso men, Loralia was able to perceive the feelings and emotions of the people around her, making it possible for her to always know what he was going through.

"I lost so much time with you."

"It was only a day, Bannack, and every moment that you suffer with that is another moment that you are taking from us. Stop thinking about what has already happened and can never be redone, and think about what has yet to happen and what could be. I love you. Nothing is going to change that."

"I love you, too," Bannack said, leaning forward to kiss her.

As she gazed back at him he realized that everything she had said she meant with her whole heart. For the first time, he let himself let go of what had happened and gave himself over completely to the powerful, consuming love that he felt for her.

7

The compound felt eerily quiet without the men. Loralia and the human women stood in the center of the compound long after the warriors had marched out of sight, disappearing into the darkness of the forest that bordered that edge of the compound. The Denynso women and the monarchs had walked away, returning to their daily activities, within just a few moments of the last man marching out of sight, but the humans and Loralia couldn't seem to pull themselves away from where they stood. These had been the spots where they were standing when their mates had given them their final kisses goodbye and stroked their faces, imparting their warmth and expressing their love even without words. They didn't want to move and break the beautiful, precious space they had created with their men.

Finally Samira sighed.

"I don't think that standing here is going to make any difference, guys. They aren't coming back today."

There was a brief pause and then the rest of the women started laughing, happily breaking the painful tension that they had all been feeling. They needed that moment, that first second that forced them to have a thought that wasn't their mates' voices and the touch of their skin. None of them wanted to do it. They all would much rather continue feeling their men close to them, but they had no idea how long it would be before the men would be back and if they didn't push themselves out of that frame of mind, they would all just allow themselves to waste away. They knew that they wouldn't be able to get through this on their own. It would take the strength of all of them to support each other and take care of the compound while their mates were gone.

"Loralia," Eden said and Loralia turned to her, "I haven't had a chance to tell you that I'm really happy that things worked out for you and Bannack."

"Thank you, Eden."

"I am, too," Zuri offered, "I heard what happened between you two and I wanted to tell you that you aren't alone."

"What do you mean?"

"I know it can feel like him being resistant to accepting you as his mate was him rejecting you, and that that can be really hurtful. I just don't want you to think that things were so easy for the rest of us."

Loralia looked at each of the women. She wasn't sure how to feel about the conversation. She had just that morning told Bannack that he needed to let go of what had happened between them at the beginning of their relationship and let them move forward into the future together, but at the same time she found it comforting to hear that these women had also coped with challenges when they were finding their way with their mates in the Denynso compound.

"It wasn't?"

"We should have told you that when we first came to see you that first night you were on the compound. It probably would have made things much easier for you," Zuri said, "The truth is that finding a mate is something that the Denynso men look forward to their entire lives, but it can be a really scary and uncomfortable experience for them. They can get really violent and aggressive, even more so than usual, and they feel like they can't get their minds straight. That's really hard for all of them, but sometimes they have a lot of their own issues to work through, too."

"I wasn't exactly the most pleasant person in the world, especially to Pyra, and basically told him that I didn't like him and didn't want anything to do with him," said Eden, giving a short laugh and looking down at her hand stroking across her belly.

"I was a virgin who was terrified of Ciyrs and had a really difficult time trusting him," Elianna offered, "and when I was kidnapped by the Klimnu, he had to deal with knowing that I was being tortured and not being able to find me."

"I had been held by the Klimnu for almost two months and tortured, and was in a coma when they brought me back to the compound," Leia said, her voice sounding strong even though it was still difficult for her to talk about her ordeal in the prison, "Gyyx spent days with me and he finally had to..." she hesitated, "excite me to get me to wake up. Even then he was terrified to touch me because I'm so small and he didn't want to hurt me."

"Ty resisted how he felt about me as hard as he could because he thought I was too young for him. I came here with Zuri when she came back to Uoria and Ty was my guide and protector. I had to force him to acknowledge that we were meant to be together."

Loralia nodded, appreciating how these women were opening up to her and feeling more confident in her new place in the compound. She turned to Zuri, the final woman in the group to tell her story. Zuri looked slightly startled as if she had forgotten that she hadn't told about her early days with her mate.

"Oh," she said, "Ero thought I was fat."

The women laughed and together they started walking back toward the houses. Loralia was processing the connection that she was feeling to these women, trying to remember what it was like to have friends to spend time with and people to rely on. She had spent so much time alone that she was finding it harder than she would have imagined just relaxing in their company and enjoying having the friendship. She knew it would take time for her to really feel like she was a part of them, but she had already begun to feel a strong loyalty to the Denynso and was looking forward to spending more time with these women.

8

———————

The acrid smell of the burned building still lingered in the air even though it had been weeks since the fire had burned the Klimnu prison to the ground. An impending storm threatening the sky had made the air feel wet and heavy, seeming to magnify the strong smell of the burned prison.

The Denynso men trudged toward the prison, all of them feeling reluctant to go back to this far corner of the compound, a site that held so many horrific memories for all of them. This had been the site of a brutal battle with the Klimnu, a clash that started when one of the creatures came into the compound disguised as Pyra and kidnapped Elianna, holding her in the prison and torturing her because they knew that her pain would radiate out to her mate, luring the rest of the Denynso to the prison so that they could attack.

The Klimnu hadn't been prepared for the fury that the warriors held that night, or the power and intensity that their actions had inspired in their healer, Ciyrs. Between the two of them, Ciyrs and Elianna had laid waste to more of the slimy creatures than a few of the warriors combined. They had hoped that it would be the end of the conflict, but, of course, it wasn't. Now as they stood only a few yards away from the black, sooty remnants of the prison, each lost in their own thoughts, it was as if they were walking into that battle again.

Bannack felt his muscles tightening as if preparing him in case he needed to attack. Around him the raindrops started to fall, cooling his skin but increasing the solemn, eerie feeling around the prison.

"Come on," he said, starting to walk toward the rubble again, "we're almost to the boundary of the compound."

They all walked toward the prison, going at an angle so that they walked around the perimeter.

"Wait," Pyra said suddenly, "What's that?"

Bannack followed the direction where he was pointing. He saw that the several rainstorms that had occurred over the weeks since their battle with the Klimnu had washed away enough of the ashes to reveal what looked like the edges of a trapdoor in the foundation. Pyra climbed into the remnants of the prison and toward the trapdoor. Bannack followed, watching carefully where he stepped to avoid stepping on something that might injure him if it suddenly gave way, broke, or splintered upwards.

By the time he had gotten to the edge of the trapdoor, Pyra was already on his knees digging with his fingers around the edge.

"Help me," he grunted.

Bannack reached forward to pull on the edge of the door. The heat from the fire seemed to have melted some of the metal, but after a few minutes of pulling, the weakened door broke and the two warriors were able to toss the pieces of door away. They stared down into what looked like a black abyss. It was so dark that they couldn't see the ground and there was no way of determining how far the fall would be between the door and the floor.

"Does anyone have a light?" Pyra asked.

Ty reached into his bag and withdrew a stick loaded with a solar power cell. Bannack took it and activated it so that it sent a wash of light down into the hole. Even with the light there wasn't anything to see. Pyra took his bag off of his shoulders and handed it to Bannack, then jumped down through the trapdoor.

"What the hell do you think you're doing?" Ero yelled, dropping to his knees beside the open trapdoor and staring down into the darkness.

Bannack swept the light back and forth until it fell on Pyra, crouched on a dark stone floor at least twenty feet down.

"It's a trapdoor," Pyra said, "It had to be close enough to the floor to let people actually get down here. Come on. Jump down."

Bannack went first, followed close by Ero. They stepped out of the way so that most of the other warriors could follow. A few had pulled out their own lights and soon there was enough illumination that they were able to see they were in some kind of dungeon.

"Well, it was close enough that we could get down, but that doesn't make any sense for the Klimnu. They're not anywhere near as big as we are. How would they get down here without breaking themselves?"

Pyra gazed up at the open trapdoor like he was pondering what Ty had just asked.

"I'm not sure. Anyway, let's look around. I didn't even know this place was here when we were here."

The group split off so that they could explore the

dungeon more efficiently, breaking up so that everyone had a light with them. They had been exploring the dark, damp hallways for nearly an hour when Ty discovered a door on an otherwise blank wall. Unlike the other doors that looked like they had once belonged to cells, this door was solid. He stepped back and directed a hard kick into the middle of the door, causing it to splinter.

Pushing aside the broken pieces of door, Ty stepped inside the small room and shined his light around. It looked like an office; a large desk on one wall, rows of bookshelves on another, and the back corner filled with what looked like stacks of drawers. Ty approached the drawers cautiously and pulled one open. It was filled with folders of documents and he pulled several out so that he could spread them across the surface of the desk.

"Hey, Pyra," he yelled a few minutes later after going through a few pages of the documents he had found in the folders.

Pyra stepped into the room and shined the light he had borrowed from another warrior after giving Ty back his on the desk.

"What did you find?"

"What do you know about this prison?" Ty asked, flipping through the fragile, aged pages of a book that looked ancient in his hands.

"Not much. I didn't even know it was here until the Klimnu attacked. I'm guessing that they built it so long ago that no one remembers it."

"I don't think they built it at all."

"What do you mean?"

"Look at this."

Pyra came around the side of the desk and Ty turned the book to show him what he was reading.

"Holy shit."

"I know."

"What's going on?" Ero asked, coming into the small room.

"This prison wasn't built by the Klimnu," Pyra told him.

"What do you mean?"

"Ty just found all of these books and papers. It looks like the Klimnu were just about as gracious with this prison as they were with the realm under the compound. Apparently this prison has been here for hundreds of years, which means that it was built before the Denynso were living on the compound."

"How could we not know that?"

"I don't know. Creia said that our kind has never made contact with other species except in battle. If it was there when the Denynso settled the compound, they either didn't notice it, or the species that built it was already gone by the time they came."

"How is that even possible?" Ero asked.

"I don't know."

"Look at this."

Pyra had pulled another, smaller book out from the stack of papers that Ty had taken out of the drawer and held it open to the other warriors. It looked almost like a military log, but was more extensive, like the person keeping it was both tracking the events and journaling about them as his way to express his thoughts and emotions.

"This says that the species that built this prison built it during a war with another species that they had been in conflict with for years. They used this prison to hold people who they captured during battle, but the other species found out and infiltrated the prison, freeing all of the captives and killing many of the Covra."

"The Covra?"

"That's what it says. I've never heard of that species before."

"What happened after that battle?"

"This says that the Covra knew that they weren't strong enough to fight off the rest of what they call the Light Ones, so they locked them."

Pyra stopped and looked up at the other men, a confused look on his face.

"Locked them?" Ty asked.

Pyra turned the page and read for a few seconds before looking up at them again.

"It says that the Covra can lock an entire area in place. It's like the whole place is frozen in time. They at once exist and don't. Time passes around them, but it doesn't impact them. They locked the entire kingdom of the Light Ones in that moment and never made any plans to release them."

Pyra met eyes with Ty, and then with Ero.

"What if they're still there?"

9

———

"What do you mean?" Ero asked.

"There's a map right here that shows where everything was when this all happened." He pointed at a large area outlined toward the upper corner of the map. "What if the kingdom is still there and the Light Ones are still stuck there, just like they have been since the Covra locked them?"

Silence fell in the room as the three men pondered what Pyra had just said. It was almost unfathomable that what that journal said could be true. After what they had all seen Loralia achieve with her mirrors, they were far more willing to accept that there were things that existed right on their own planet that they didn't understand, and species that could accomplish truly astounding things. The idea that one of these creatures could literally stop time for an entire other species, and that that frozen kingdom could still be persisting in its fully locked state just as it had been for years was too much for any of them to wrap their minds around.

"Pyra?"

The voice of another of the warriors made them all turn to the door to the office. Lynx stood there, leaning into the room with the glow from the light in his hand directed at the floor.

"What is it, Lynx?" Pyra asked.

There really isn't much down here. A bunch of cells. A couple of old chains."

"Tell the men to find a way to get back up out of the trapdoor and gather up outside. Our little adventure here is taking a detour."

"Where are we going?"

"Back in time, it looks like."

TWENTY MINUTES later the men had managed to find a nearly rusted-out metal ladder that looked like it was once attached to the bottom of the trapdoor so it could be used to climb in and out of the dungeon and had gathered right outside in the soft rain. Though the fact that the Klimnu had not actually built the prison originally explained why the structure was built as it was, the existence of the ladder seemed to make the dungeon make more sense.

Pyra gave them a brief overview of what they had found out in the office in the dungeon and told them that they were going to follow that map and see what they could find in the place that marked where the kingdom of the Light Ones at least once stood. Lynx watched him push the stack of papers and books he had carried out of the dungeon into the bag that he had returned to his hip and headed out toward the furthest boundary of the compound, past the wastelands and toward the complete unknown.

The rain intensified as they walked, starting to beat down on them in stinging streams that hurt as they bit into

Lynx's exposed skin. It was that fearsome type of rain that made you want to stay inside, drink something hot, and wait until it was over. The men didn't have that option, now. They had committed themselves to this mission, and now it seemed to be taking on even more meaning that it had when they had first started. When he first agreed to go along with them to explore Uoria, Lynx never would have imagined that they would be gone from their homes for only a few hours and already have learned of two species that they didn't know existed up until that point, but also a whole history of the planet and their own compound that none of them had known.

Though he hated himself for thinking it, and wouldn't ever have admitted it in those first few hours, Lynx was starting to change his perception of Creia. Like the other warriors, he had been raised believing that this man was the most powerful and wise of all of the Denynso. Part of a bloodline known for their extraordinary longevity, he had ruled for many decades and had faced many of the earliest battles and conflicts in the ranks of the warriors. It had been Creia who had shown the strength and courage to banish the Klimnu because of their greedy, vicious ways rather than letting them intimidate him into helping them. With all of this history and knowledge, however, he somehow hadn't known about the mirrored realm that existed just beneath the compound he had called home his entire life, or about the prison in the wastelands.

At least, he told them that he didn't know. The longer that they walked, the more footsteps that they put between the area of the compound that they knew and themselves, the more Lynx wondered how honest Creia had really been with them. Was it possible that he had known about the prison and the apparently brutal, drawn-out conflict that had existed there so long ago? Had he been completely honest with them when he told them that their kind had not made contact with others outside of the battles waged on the soil of their own compound?

Lynx felt painfully guilty for even entertaining those thoughts for a second. As a Denynso warrior, it was his responsibility and birthright to honor, respect, and obey Creia without question. He was meant to follow him and do as he ordered no matter what. The thought of questioning him for even a second would be something that the other warriors, or the king himself, would never have tolerated.

The young warrior was so lost in his own thoughts that he didn't notice the rest of the warriors had stopped and he ran directly into Gyyx's back. The larger, older warriors turned and glared at him, but turned back to face ahead of him without saying anything. Lynx stepped around to stand beside Gyyx and looked to where Pyra was standing several feet in front of the rest of them. A tall wall of weathered, ancient rocks stood just in front of him. It was the far boundary of the Denynso compound, laid by the very hands of the first of the clan. They had built in there to protect all who lived within it, intending, as the warriors had all been taught from the time that they were little children, that none would ever come inside the boundary to take the compound from them, no species not welcomed by the Denynso would come within the space without quick and brutal retribution, and that none of their kind would ever step beyond it.

They were prepared now to break free of those restraints; to be the first to go past the boundary and take back the freedom of existence on the entirety of the planet of Uoria.

10

———

"This is your last chance, men," Pyra said, his voice rumbling through the silence that had formed around them, "Once we go over this wall, we are out of the compound and facing things that none of us know or understand. There will be no turning back. If you aren't ready to do this, tell us now and you can go back. Think very hard about your decision, because it is one of the most important that you will ever make."

Pyra's glowing orange eyes burned into each of the men, giving them time to think about the implications of moving beyond that boundary and walking out onto the rest of the planet. Though they were feared throughout the galaxy, each of them was very aware that the compound had protected them, had guarded them. When they went beyond that wall, there was nothing left to surround them and keep them safe. Of course, that wall had also failed them when it came to keeping the Klimnu from attacking and tormenting them. It hadn't been enough to prevent the betrayal of the traitor Ullie, and it hadn't guarded them from the work of the flight attendant who had cooperated

with him and the slimy, disgusting Klimnu to nearly spell
the end of the Denynso.

Lynx could feel that the rest of the warriors around him
felt the same way. They could no longer put their total blind
trust and confidence in that wall. It was time that they took
responsibility for themselves.

When none of the men told him that they wanted to
turn back, Pyra nodded at them, his face not smiling but
carrying an expression that offered a hint of strength and
pride. He tilted his head back to evaluate the wall and then
reached onto the side of his bag to untie a grappling hook.
The other men followed suit, taking their hooks from their
bags and preparing the ropes. A few moments later the
Denynso stood in a long line in front of the wall.

At Pyra's command, they swung their hooks over the top
of the wall and waited until they felt them catch in the
stones on the other side. Moving in the perfect, nearly
choreographed rhythm they had trained into their ranks,
the men used the pressure of the hooks and the strength of
the ropes to steady them as they climbed up the wall.

Lynx stopped when he reached the top of the wall and
gazed out over the land that lay on the other side. It looked
much like the far areas of the compound where there were
no buildings or roads, but somehow despite its similarities,
it still seemed sparser and unwelcoming.

Not wanting to be the last to be off the wall, Lynx
dropped down on the other side of the wall and went
through the same procedure as all of the other men,
recoiling their hooks and attaching them back to their bags
for use the next time that they may need them. Pyra didn't
say another word, but waited until all of the men had come
over the wall, and then started further along the open field.
Lynx could see his gaze focused intensely on the stands of

trees that dotted the field and the tall, coarse grass to either side of them. It was as though their leader were on edge with every footstep, just waiting for something to come out at them.

Pyra consulted the map in the book in his hand every few minutes, occasionally calling back to the rest of the men about which direction they needed to go, or about how far he thought it would be. Lynx followed silently, preferring to keep himself vigilant about what may be lurking at any corner rather than responding when any of the men spoke.

They had been walking for what felt like hours when Pyra suddenly slowed and all of the men followed his gaze to a towering, ivy-covered stone archway a few yards ahead of them. A worn, crumbling stone wall very similar to the one that they had crossed to leave the compound but older and of darker-colored rocks stretched out to either side of the archway and Lynx could see that it, too, had been taken over by the plants of the area that seemed to be trying to reclaim that space.

"This is it," Pyra said almost under his breath, "I can't believe it's actually here."

The men stood in stunned silence for several long seconds, not entirely sure of what they should do from there. They had come this far looking for the kingdom to see if it actually existed, and now that they had found that it did, and that it was still there, they didn't know what to do next.

"Are we going inside?" Ero asked.

Lynx watched Pyra nod.

"The only way to find out if all of this about the Covra and the Light Ones is real is to go in there and see if we find a kingdom that has been locked in time."

"How do we know that if it is all real, that we will be able to go in there at all, or that if we can, that we won't get locked too?" Ty asked.

"We don't," Pyra responded simply, "We don't know any of that. We can't just walk away from it, though. The whole point of us leaving the compound was to find out what else existed on this planet. Well, this is what else exists here. We can't stop now. We have to keep going and find out exactly what happened in there, and what is still happening, whether that means that all of the stuff in these books was just a bunch of made-up stories and that is an abandoned archway to an empty kingdom that no one has lived in for centuries, or that it is all absolutely true and waiting right inside there is an entire species that hasn't changed in longer than any of us have been alive."

"What if something does happen to us, though?" asked one of the warriors from the back of the group, "What about Eden and the baby?"

Pyra's eyes flashed at the mention of his mate and their unborn child and Lynx saw his back straighten and his shoulders square forcefully.

"My mate trusts me. She put her faith in me to find out more about Uoria so that I will be able to protect her and our baby well into the future. As for the baby, my child will know that I didn't stop at anything to make sure that my family was safe, and that I never cowered away from a challenge or a risk. I never want to look my baby in the eye and know that I didn't do absolutely everything that I could to complete my goal out here."

"And if we do find the so-called Light Ones in there," Ciyrs interjected, "there is a possibility that we could help them. They might not have to be locked forever."

As if this conversation propelled him, Pyra suddenly took off running, closing the space between himself and the archway in a matter of seconds. Ero, Ty, Gyyx, and Ciyrs followed closely after. That is when Lynx started running. Closing his eyes briefly against the fear that had settled into his stomach, he pushed himself to run as fast and as hard as he could, crossing through the archway mere seconds after Pyra had disappeared beneath the stone.

As soon as he passed through the archway, Lynx slowed and stopped. He looked up and for a moment he was afraid that Ero had been right and that they had all been locked right along with the kingdom and the Light Ones within it. Soon, though, he realized that he could think and move and he took a few more steps into the kingdom, gazing around with a sense of absolute awe. It was as if he had stepped into a painting.

11

―――――

The kingdom somewhat resembled their compound, with what looked like rows of houses along a main road and a larger building positioned in the distance. Everything seemed more tightly positioned than the compound, however, and there was a greater sense of formality. Rather than the soft dirt that covered the roads in the Denynso compound, the roads here were covered in broken rocks that had been smoothed around the edges to fit in close together. The houses looked larger and more elaborate, too, with strange design elements that Lynx didn't understand.

What was undoubtedly the most fascinating part of the kingdom that they now wandered into, however, was the people. All around them were still, silent people, their bodies shaped into the postures of normal life, but none of them moved or breathed. It truly looked like they had been stopped, crystallized into a single second of their existence, and had not moved since.

"Everyone spread out," Pyra said evenly, slipping the book that held the map to the kingdom into his bag so that his hands were free, "Explore as much of the area as you can, but make sure that you keep contact with at least one other of us. We don't need anybody getting lost."

At that command, the men slowly dissipated, wandering in their own direction further into the kingdom as if each of them were drawn toward a certain place. It was unnerving to see the people scattered through the space, their eyes open but unseeing, their bodies primed for action but unable to move. There was a large garden in the center of the houses and Lynx saw several people in it, tending to crops that were still perfect after all this time. One woman leaned over, her hand just cupped around a vegetable she intended to pick while a man nearby rested with his arms crossed on top of a tall gardening implement. Lynx sighed, musing that that man could not have imagined how long his break was actually going to be when he stopped his work on that fateful day.

To one side Lynx could see a small group of children playing, locked in their laughter and joy, and he had to turn away. It was too painful to see the innocence of little ones stolen from them because of a war between adults, a conflict that they would never understand.

Turning his back toward the children, Lynx walked toward one of the houses. It drew him in in a way that the others didn't, and he felt compelled to go inside. He called out to Ty who he saw walking along at the end of the street, letting him know that he was going inside the house so that someone knew where he was should the rest of the men decide to leave the kingdom before he got out of the house, or if there was something inside that might threaten him.

He didn't expect the door to open as easily beneath his hand as it did. When it opened fully, he stepped inside the cool, airy house and looked around. Just as the outsides of the homes were more complex in their design than the Denynso homes back on the compound, they were more complex on the inside as well. Multiple rooms stretched out from the front entryway, and a set of stairs headed up to another floor. He followed his instincts and let them pull him to the stairs, keeping him focused on the landing above him as he climbed them.

At the top of the stairs Lynx let the strange, tight feeling in his belly guide him toward a room at the center of the hallway. The door was partially open and when he pushed it the rest of the way open, he felt his heart constrict.

It was a bedroom with pale yellow walls, airy white curtains on the window, and a large canopy bed tucked in one corner. On that bed lay the most beautiful woman that Lynx had ever seen, and as soon as his eyes rested on the long strands of coppery hair spread across the pillow, her pale, delicate face, and full, pink lips, he felt everything inside him unravel as an overwhelming sense of love, desire, and the need to protect her took over.

Lynx walked cautiously to the side of the bed and gazed down at her face, so perfect and calm in the sleep in which she had been locked. It made no sense, but he felt completely and inarguably in love with her, the same intense, immediate feeling of soul-wrenching attraction and need that the other men had described when talking about meeting their mates. This was a woman who had lived generations before he was even born, and yet Lynx felt inextricably connected to her, as if all this time she had been lying here sleeping, waiting for him to come find her.

Something on the nightstand beside her bed caught Lynx's eye and he picked up a silver-framed picture that looked like a younger version of the woman in the bed standing with two older people in front of a large house that resembled the houses along the main street, but much larger. Lynx flipped the frame over in his hand and released the brackets that held the picture in place. When the backing came off of the frame, he rested it carefully on the nightstand and took the picture out so that he could look at the back.

Visit to the homeland
Earth
Rain, 22 years

LYNX GASPED as he realized what the inscription meant. These were not some strange, unknown species that they had never encountered. These were creatures with whom the Denynso were becoming quite familiar.

The Light Ones were humans.

Taking the picture with the intention of showing it to Pyra, Lynx took a final look at the beautiful woman, whose name he could only guess to be Rain, and then turned to the door to leave. Before he could take another step, however, a series of deathly sharp black spikes came around the doorframe, cutting into the wall as they gripped into it to pull massive black bodies like gruesome spiders into the room and toward Lynx.

TBC

(To be continued in Part IV...)

www.ingramcontent.com/pod-product-compliance
Lightning Source LLC
Chambersburg PA
CBHW032044180726
48284CB00008B/2745